WHAT'S THE MATTER WITH HERBIE JONES?

Ray peered sadly through the glass door. He saw Herbie and Annabelle laughing. Herbie didn't even care that he was gone. They sure don't need me, he thought.

Ray wanted to cry, but he didn't. He hugged Shadow, his dog, instead. What was the matter with Herbie, anyway? Was he sick or something?

Then Ray noticed they had stopped laughing. Herbie's green notebook slipped off the table and fell on the floor. When both of them stooped down to get it, their heads bumped.

Annabelle blushed.

Herbie was only inches from Annabelle's eyes. He just stared into them and didn't move.

Ray jumped up! Oh no, he thought. Ray knew what was wrong with Herbie. He was sick all right. Lovesick. Herbie Jones liked a girl. Herbie Jones had the girl disease, the G disease!

Ray couldn't desert his buddy now. He had to keep a closer watch on things, and just maybe there was time to save him before it was too late.

W9-CJU-028

What's the Matter with HERBIE JONES?

by Suzy Kline

ILLUSTRATED BY RICHARD WILLIAMS

SCHOLASTIC INC.
New York Toronto London Auckland Sydney
Mexico City New Delhi Hong Kong Buenos Aires

Acknowledgements

Special thanks to my editor, Anne O'Connell

"Fog" by Carl Sandburg from *Chicago Poems*, copyright © 1916 by Holt, Rinehart and Winston; renewed 1944 by Carl Sandburg. Reprinted by permission of Harcourt Brace Jovanovich, Inc.

ISBN 0-439-31858-0

12 11 10 9 8 7 6 5 4 3 2 1   2 3 4 5 6 7/0

Printed in the U.S.A.   40

First Scholastic printing, January 2002

Set in Caledonia

To Rufus with love
Again, thank you for your insights

Contents

What's the Matter with
Herbie Jones?

1

The Ghost of Annabelle

Herbie Jones rang the doorbell.

He didn't want to be the one to do this, but his third grade teacher, Miss Pinkham, said he had to because he lived around the corner. Margie Sherman was supposed to do it, but she was sent home from school with a fever.

Herbie looked at the Siamese cat sitting on the porch. He didn't look very friendly.

Herbie rang the doorbell again.

A tall, thin man with glasses answered. "Why hello, Herbie."

"Hello, Mr. Hodgekiss. I brought Annabelle some Get Well cards from our class. Here. Would you please give them to her?" Herbie figured he had done his job so he turned around and headed down the steps.

"Just a minute, Herbie. Won't you come in and give the cards to Annabelle yourself? The doctor said she isn't contagious anymore."

Herbie stopped cold.

He was just supposed to deliver them to the door.

Not go in.

Miss Pinkham never said he had to do that.

Anyway, he and Annabelle Louisa Hodgekiss weren't even talking to each other.

Ever since the poster contest for Mr. D's Card Shop in town, Annabelle had decided not to talk to anyone in the class who didn't raise their hand for her daisy poster. Herbie had voted for his best friend Raymond Martin's poster, the one with the Viking ship.

Herbie remembered how quickly Annabelle took out her memo cube with her initials ALH on it and recorded names. His name was the first one on the list, AND it had three checks after it.

"Just for a minute?" Mr. Hodgekiss repeated.

Herbie was trapped. He half nodded and walked into the house. He felt his throat getting dry and raspy.

Herbie sure didn't like going into a girl's bedroom. His sister's was barricaded with signs like DO NOT ENTER! DO NOT DISTURB!, GENIUS AT WORK! and BEWARE OF DOG! Herbie thought the last sign was dumb. They didn't have a dog.

When he got to Annabelle's door, he noticed how clean and white it was. There wasn't even one poster tacked on it.

Mr. Hodgekiss turned to Herbie. "Before we go in, I must tell you something. Annabelle has been very stubborn about having the chicken pox."

Herbie's answer squeaked like a frog. "Re-aaally?" He tried to act surprised, but the fact was, Herbie already knew Annabelle was stubborn—about everything.

Mr. Hodgekiss took his glasses off and wiped them with a crisp white handkerchief. "She insists on putting her sheet over her head every time someone other than her mother goes into her room. She won't even let ME see her face. She says when the spots and scabs are gone in a few days, she won't hide behind the sheet."

"No kidding?" Herbie replied. He liked the idea of visiting someone with a sheet over her head. It was like visiting a ghost—the ghost of Annabelle. "When is she coming back to school?" Herbie hoped she'd wear her sheet to class.

"Friday. I guess there is something important going on that day at school."

"Oh, yeah . . ." Herbie mumbled, half listening. He was still picturing what it would be like to sit next to a ghost in class. It was a neat idea, he thought.

"Well . . . maybe you'll have better luck with her," Mr. Hodgekiss continued. Then he knocked on Annabelle's door. "Dear, may we come in?"

"Who's with you?"

"Someone from school. He has some Get Well cards for you." Mr. Hodgekiss opened the door slowly.

Herbie saw Annabelle sitting up in bed. The sheet was tucked behind her head.

"Who is it?" she asked again.

Mr. Hodgekiss bent over and picked some green lint off the bedroom carpet. "See for yourself, dear." Then he walked out, smiling at Herbie.

Herbie quickly looked around the room. He noticed the daisy poster hanging on the wall. The blue ribbon was still on it.

Herbie sat down at Annabelle's desk. He felt a tickle in his throat, "Hi . . . hi, Annabelle."

"Do you have a cold, John, or is that your asthma acting up again?"

John?

Hey, this could be fun, Herbie thought. Here he was visiting a ghost, and now he could even pretend he was someone else. "Just . . . just my asthma," Herbie replied, clearing his voice. He decided not to say too much. He didn't want to spoil the game.

"Did you bring me some cards?"

"Yup." Herbie looked at Annabelle. He could barely make out her nose and eye sockets, but when she said something, the sheet puffed out from her lips. Herbie thought she made kind of a cute ghost, if you could call a girl cute.

"Here's two," Herbie said, pulling them out of a Manila folder.

"Read them to me," Annabelle asked.

"Sure," Herbie said as he placed the folder on her bookcase. He noticed the books were arranged alphabetically by author, and that they were all chapter books.

"Here's one with a Viking ship on it."

"I know, that's from Raymond Martin. He always draws Viking ships."

"Yup, and on the inside it says, BON VOYAGE!"

"BON VOYAGE?" The sheet billowed around her lips.

Herbie remembered seeing those words on cards at Mr. D's. The cards were Ray's favorites because they had ships and planes on them.

Annabelle shook her head. "That's dumb. Bon Voyage means have a good trip. Having the chicken pox is NOT having fun, and you certainly can't go anywhere!"

Herbie shrugged. He thought staying out of school for a week would be fun. Then he remem-

bered to cough a few times and act like John.

"Here's a real nice card. It has you in bed with your cat and a thermometer in your mouth."

"Hmm, I wonder who made that one?"

"It even has a poem inside." Herbie began reading:

Annabelle, Annabelle,
  sick in bed
Spots on her nose
And spots on her head
Think I will give her a
  brite red rose
Then she nos
  I will tickel her toes
With it.

Annabelle giggled so much her sheet shook. "That's funny! Who wrote it?"

Herbie tipped back his chair: "Herbie Jones."

Annabelle straightened up. "Herbie Jones wrote THAT?"

"The one and only," Herbie said proudly.

Annabelle was quiet for a moment. Then her cat, Sukey, jumped up on the bed, and she started petting his fur. "Well . . . you know, John."

"Yes, Annabelle . . ." Herbie was enjoying this.

"I'm not speaking to Herbie . . ."

"Uh huh . . ."

"And it's not just because he didn't vote for my daisy poster."

"Oh?" Herbie wondered if he was going to find out why his name had three checks after it.

"Herbie Jones wore earrings to school in October!"

Herbie counted one check to himself.

"It was Halloween," Annabelle continued, "and he was supposed to be a pirate. Everyone knows a pirate wears just one *gold* earring. Herbie wore a pair of strawberries."

Herbie remembered. It was the first pair he found. He didn't want to hang around his sister's room for too long. She'd kill him for getting into her jewelry.

" . . .and," Annabelle went on, "he wrote a story at Thanksgiving time about a turkey who got his head chopped off, and he called the turkey Annabelle."

Herbie grinned. The story was one of his favorites. That was check two, he figured.

". . . and he gave me a can of salmon for my birthday."

Check three. What a memory, Herbie thought. He decided to leave. It was getting dangerous. He figured he had played John long enough.

"But," Annabelle added as she smoothed her sheet, "Herbie Jones does have a way with words."

Herbie stopped at the door. "Herbie Jones has a way with words?"

"IF YOU TELL HERBIE I SAID THAT, JOHN GREENWEED, I'LL KILL YOU!"

Herbie snatched a Kleenex from the flowered box on her desk and held it up to his mouth. This was no time to be discovered now. "I won't," Herbie said talking into the tissue. "Your secret is safe with me."

Mr. Hodgekiss saw Herbie to the door. "Did she talk to you face to face?"

21

"No," Herbie said, feeling somewhat guilty. "She even thinks . . . I'm . . . John Greenweed. I kind of went along with it . . . in fun."

Herbie wondered if he was going to get in trouble.

"Listen, Herbie, if my daughter wants to play games, other people can too. Your secret is safe with me, *John*." He winked.

Herbie smiled. He was glad Mr. Hodgekiss had a sense of humor.

As Herbie shuffled along the sidewalk, he kept thinking about what Annabelle had said: "Herbie Jones does have a way with words."

Was that really true? Herbie decided he would have to do some experimenting.

2

Poems and the Foolproof Plan

That week after dinner, Herbie sat at the kitchen table writing. On Thursday, he started in before dinner when his thirteen-year-old sister Olivia was trying to set the table.

"Mom will be home in twenty minutes from Dipping Donuts, will you please move, and HELP?"

"A poet doesn't set the table. He's too busy writing on it," Herbie said.

Olivia sat down and folded her hands. "Read me one of your gems."

"Sure . . . Here's one I just finished:

Spigetti is red
Meatballs are brown
You make them with eggs
And a pound of ground round

Olivia stood up and continued folding napkins. "We make our meatballs with plain hamburger. Ground round is too expensive."

"One more poem?" Herbie asked.

"Just *one*, I've got lots to do."

Let's go home
Someones on the phone
Lift up the reseaver
It's Mr. Weaver
Let's go home

Olivia stopped folding napkins. "Who's Mr. Weaver?"

Herbie shrugged. "I had to have somebody that rhymed with receiver."

"I can see you give your poetry lots of thought and feeling."

"Yeah?"

Before Olivia could explain to Herbie that she was kidding, Mrs. Jones bounded in the back door. "Hi kids! I'm home."

She had a grocery bag in her arms. "Boy, am I tired. I must have served 1,000 cups of coffee today and more donuts than I want to think about."

She sat down on a kitchen chair and took off her white shoes. As she propped her feet on a chair, she motioned to Olivia. "Would you put these groceries away for me, dear? My feet are killing me."

Herbie peeked into the bag. There was the purple and white shiny sack. Day old donuts. That was the best part of having his mom work at Dipping Donuts. She always brought some home free.

Olivia grabbed the bag and gave Herbie a dirty look.

"I've got a poem I'd like to read to you, Mom," he said.

"Wonderful. Read it to me. It might soothe my nerves."

25

Olivia banged around in the pantry while Herbie read some of his poetry.

When the sun is yellow
It's time to play.
    When the sun is red,
It's time to go to bed.

Mrs. Jones clapped her hands. "Another fun poem!"

Olivia stuck her head in the kitchen. She had a can of sauerkraut in her hand. "You mean *dumb* poem. It doesn't make sense. We go to bed when it's dark. The sun isn't even out."

"I know, I know," Herbie explained, "but I needed . . ."

". . . a word to rhyme with red," Olivia finished.

"How did you know?" Herbie asked.

"That's enough, Olivia," Mrs. Jones replied. "Be encouraging. Your brother is interested in writing poetry." And then she got up and went into the living room.

"He should read some real poetry then!" Olivia said as the phone rang. She picked it up on the second ring.

"For you, Herbie. It's . . . it's Mr. Weaver."

Herbie made a face and then grabbed the phone from his sister. "Hello? Hey, Ray, what's up?"

"Herbie? Where have you been? I've been waiting for over an hour. We have important business to do, remember?"

Herbie had completely forgotten that he was supposed to be at Raymond Martin's house.

He also forgot what for. "Okay, I can come over for a little while . . . before dinner."

Herbie walked down Washington Avenue and then crossed Fish Street. When he got to Wainwright Crescent, he took a right. Ray's house was the second one from the library. It was the only one on the block that needed painting. The grass was the tallest, and two overgrown shrubs covered most of the front porch.

Herbie skipped two steps and knocked on the door. He knew the doorbell wasn't working.

Mrs. Martin answered. She was short with brown, curly hair like Raymond. "Hi, Herbie, come on in. Ray's upstairs in his room."

"Hi, Mrs. Martin. How are you?"

"Terrible. I have a headache that won't go away."

"Sorry about that." Herbie walked across the dark living room. He noticed how messy it was and that the curtains were closed. Mrs. Martin never opened her curtains. Probably because the house was messy, Herbie thought.

Herbie raced upstairs and headed for Ray's bedroom. He knew which door. He had been to Ray's house lots of times. It was the one with the sign, ROBERT'S ROOM.

Ray had wanted to pick out a sign with his own name, but the only two on sale were ROBERT'S ROOM and MARY'S ROOM. He definitely didn't want the MARY'S ROOM sign.

Herbie stepped over a big, black dog sleeping in Ray's doorway. "Good boy, Shadow," Herbie said, giving him a pat on the back.

"So . . ." Herbie said, plopping down on Ray's unmade bed, "what's so important?"

"You mean you forgot?"

Herbie looked puzzled. "What?"

"Tomorrow is Friday, remember?"

Friday . . . Friday . . . Herbie remembered Mr. Hodgekiss saying something about that being a big day for Annabelle. "What about Friday?"

"Herbie, tomorrow is the dance contest. We were supposed to come up with a foolproof plan to get out of it this afternoon, remember?"

Herbie fell back on the bed. His feet flipped in the air. "Oh . . . no!"

"What have you been doing since three o'clock, anyway?"

Herbie glanced up at Ray's ceiling. There was a daddy-longlegs walking across it. "I've been writing poems. I forgot all about that dumb dance contest."

"What are you writing poems for?"

"It's fun. Want to write some together?"

"No way. The only writing I do is when some-

29

one tells me I have to, like Miss Pinkham or my mother."

Herbie sat up. "Your mom makes you write?"

"You know. At Christmas time when you have to write thank you notes, and when it's someone's birthday, I have to sign my name on the card."

Herbie looked disappointed. He thought it would be fun to write a poem about the daddy-longlegs, but Ray wouldn't understand.

"So, Herbie, let's get down to our important business. How do we get out of that dance contest tomorrow? Miss Pinkham even said it's going to have three parts to it."

"That's deadly."

"Yeah."

"Well," Herbie replied, "we need a foolproof plan."

The room turned quiet while the boys thought.

Suddenly Herbie stood up and snapped his fingers. "I GOT IT!" he said.

"You do?"

"Listen, Miss Pinkham always has a boy-ask-girl when we dance in the gym."

"Yeah . . ."

"Well, with Sarah Sitwellington out with the chicken pox, there will be thirteen girls and fifteen boys."

Ray did some quick math. "That means there will be two extra boys!"

"Right! So what we do is walk real slow, like snails, and when we get to the other side . . ."

"BINGO!" Ray shrieked. "NO PARTNERS!"

Herbie leaped into the air and then onto the bed. "YAHOO!" he shouted.

"YEE HAW!" Ray screeched as he dived on the bed.

"WHOOO-EEE!" Herbie yelled.

Shadow woke up and jumped on the bed too. Then he started barking.

"See," Ray said. "Shadow is happy about it too."

Mrs. Martin appeared at the door with a plastic bottle in her hand. "Please boys, no noise . . . I have this splitting headache, and I can't get these silly aspirins out of the bottle."

Herbie got up. He noticed she wasn't having much luck pulling the cotton out. "I can do that for you," he offered.

"You can?"

31

Herbie reached in his back pocket for his pair of tweezers. He used them to pull out the wad of cotton. "There," he said, "no problem."

"Amazing," Mrs. Martin replied. "You carry those things with you all the time?"

"Yup, they're my Trusty Tweezers. See the name printed on the side here?" Herbie held them up so she could see the words: TRUSTY TWEEZERS.

"Hmm," she mumbled.

"I use them for lots of things, right Ray?"

"Right, like picking up spiders and their egg sacs, and worms, and . . ."

Mrs. Martin began to wince. "That's fine, dear. I think I'll lie down now. Thank you, Herbie, for your help."

Herbie put his Trusty Tweezers back in his pocket and left. Now that he and Ray had a foolproof plan for the dance contest tomorrow, he could get back to writing some more poetry.

3

The Dance Contest

When the bell rang Friday and the students were in their seats, Miss Pinkham welcomed back Annabelle. Then she reminded the class that the dance contest was at one-thirty in the gym. She also said she was pleased that all the girls remembered to wear dresses or skirts and that most of the boys remembered to wear ties.

Everyone looked at Herbie and Raymond.

They were the only boys who forgot.

After the pledge and the moment of silence, Herbie raised his hand. "I have something for our morning conversation."

"You do, Herbie?" Miss Pinkham replied.

"I've been experimenting with writing poems. I thought maybe I could read one. It's called 'Spring.'"

Miss Pinkham sat down on a student's desk and folded her hands. "Wonderful! Come up in front of the class so we can all hear you."

Herbie took out his thick green notebook—it was half full now—and walked up the aisle.

As he brushed by Annabelle and her yellow flowered dress, she smiled. "I liked your Get Well card," she whispered.

So . . . she was talking to him now, Herbie thought. It must have been the power of his poetry.

Herbie stood before the class. If he had remembered to wear his Sunday tie, he would have straightened it. He began reading.

Daffidills yellow
Daffidills sweet,
Grow in my garden
Down by my feet
Spring is here
Spring is fun
If you spray me with the hose
I'll sqirt you with my water gun.

The class laughed. Miss Pinkham clapped and then everyone else did too. "We enjoyed your poem, Herbie, thank you."

At one-thirty, Miss Pinkham led the class briskly down to the gym in two straight, quiet lines. She had the girls stand on one side of the gym and the boys on the other.

"Today we have our first dance contest. Our thanks go to Margie Sherman for making the paper trophies . . ."

The children clapped.

". . . and to all of you for learning the dance steps so well this year. I've asked our cook, Mrs. Coffey, to sit in and do the judging. Thank you, Mrs. Coffey."

Mrs. Coffey waved from her chair next to the record player. "It's nice to get out of the kitchen for a break!" she said.

The children clapped again.

"Now . . . we'll have a boys' choice," Miss Pinkham announced.

Ray looked at Herbie. Things were going perfectly according to plan.

Then Annabelle Louisa Hodgekiss raised her hand. "May I make a quick suggestion, Miss Pinkham, before we start?"

"Of course, what is it?"

"Every time we have dancing, we have a boys' choice. Can't we have a girls' choice for a change?"

Ray looked at Herbie again. This time Herbie shook his head. This was NOT supposed to happen. Even John Greenweed, who was standing next to Herbie, got nervous. He took out his empty inhalator and fiddled with it.

"I think that's a splendid idea! I should have thought of it myself. Routine can do that to a teacher."

Mrs. Coffey nodded in agreement.

"Yes." Miss Pinkham raised her voice. "Let's have a girls' choice! Our first number is a square dance."

Herbie felt sick.

Raymond tied his tennis shoe.

The girls ran across the floor. They reminded Herbie of attacking Indians. All they needed were tomahawks, he thought.

Annabelle and Margie were the first two girls to make it across the gym floor.

Annabelle stood directly in front of John Green-weed. "Shall we dance?" she said.

Before John could give a reply, he started wheezing and coughing.

"John, you sound like you did when you stopped by with those . . ."

Herbie looked over. He couldn't believe his ears! Annabelle was going to tell John about the Get Well cards!

He was doomed. This was an emergency. Maybe even the kind his father called *dire*.

And emergencies called for drastic measures.

Herbie stepped in front of Annabelle and grabbed her arm. "Let's dance, Annabelle, John should see the nurse."

"Herbie Jones, what *are* you doing?"

Herbie knew he had to do some fast talking. He was just glad no one was close enough to hear. "Annabelle, you looked so pretty in that yellow dress, I just HAD to dance with you!"

Annabelle was quiet. For a moment.

37

Then she started in again. "This was SUP-
POSED to be a girl-ask-boy, and I was SUP-
POSED to dance with John. John is the best
dancer in our class. I don't want to be stuck with
you in a dance contest. You *hate* to dance!"

"Me? Hate dancing? No. You're dead wrong."

"I am?"

"Wait a minute, Annabelle." Herbie looked
around to make sure he wouldn't be heard. "I've
even had dance lessons."

"Dance lessons?"

"Yeah, my mom put me in a . . . a ballet class."

"When?"

Herbie lowered his voice. "When I was three."

"Funny. Listen Herbie, you better dance your
very best because I want to win this contest."

Herbie held up his arm. "Annabelle," he said,
"you haven't seen anything yet!" And then Herbie
led Annabelle out to a square and bowed. Annabelle grasped the skirt of her yellow dress and
curtsied.

"Do-si-do your partner!" Miss Pinkham shouted
as she turned on the Virginia Reel record.

38

Herbie do-si-doed Annabelle. Her yellow ribbons brushed against his cheeks.

"Swing that pretty gal!" Miss Pinkham continued as she and Mrs. Coffey clapped their hands.

Herbie swung Annabelle holding his arm strongly crooked. He had made up his mind that he could dance as well as John or anybody else. Annabelle wasn't going to lose this dance contest on account of him.

"Down the center, Virginia Reel!" Miss Pinkham called out.

One by one the couples met at the head of the square and sashayed down the center, laughing.

Herbie decided to forget his hatred for dancing temporarily, because to his surprise he thought it was kind of fun. He even shouted "YEE HAW!" at the top of the square. Halfway down the center, Herbie lifted his right arm high so that Annabelle could twirl underneath. He remembered seeing two ice skaters do that step on TV. Everyone clapped.

"The second dance will be a disco. So do your own thing!" Miss Pinkham said as she put on a new record. Miss Pinkham could be fun, especially with dancing. She must have liked disco, because Herbie could see her foot tapping.

During the disco is when Herbie really cut loose. He swayed from side to side. He threw his arms in the air and bounced with the beat. Annabelle had never seen Herbie Jones dance like that before. She was not to be outdone, though. She dipped and shifted her weight from side to side too and made a few dazzling turns and spins.

Miss Pinkham clapped.

Mrs. Coffey shouted, "Bravo!"

"And now, boys and girls, the third and final dance will be the one I taught you just last month. The box step. Just remember, it goes: side-together-forward AND side-together-back; side-together-forward AND side-together-back."

Miss Pinkham put on a record. It was a slow one.

Herbie slipped his right arm around Annabelle's waist and held her hand with his left. Then he carefully moved his left foot forward to guide her into a perfect box step. Both of them got in step from the start, and that made it easier. Herbie was close enough to Annabelle to smell her hair, which

reminded him of his mother's gardenia bush planted next to the garbage can. Annabelle had never followed Herbie in anything before, but she did during the box step. She completely forgot about not dancing with John. She wanted to concentrate on the "side-together-forward" and "side-together-back."

Herbie Jones was never the same.

They won the dance contest. Mrs. Coffey handed them each a paper-cup trophy to take home. Herbie didn't care about the trophy. What he did care about was the fact that he had danced with Annabelle Louisa Hodgekiss.

Raymond shook his head on the way home from school. "Well, Herbie, our foolproof plan sure backfired. I had to dance with Margie Sherman and you . . . you had to dance with Annabelle Louisa Hodgekiss. Feel sick?"

Herbie seemed to be in a trance.

"Yo, Herbie! Are you there?"

Herbie shook his head. "Huh?"

"Feel sick from dancing with a girl?"

"No. It was kind of . . . fun."

"You all right, Herbie?"

"Of course. I'm fine."

"Good, let's go to my house for some fizzy lemonade."

"Gee, Ray, Annabelle asked me to go to her house and write a few poems."

"She did?"

Herbie nodded.

"And you're GOING?"

Herbie nodded again, and then waved goodbye as he turned up Fish Street.

Raymond watched his buddy. Wanting to spend the afternoon writing poems was bad enough. But getting mixed up with a girl like Annabelle was trouble, he thought.

Ray decided he would have to keep an eye out for his best friend.

4

Under the Library Table

"Herbie! Your dinner's getting cold," Mrs. Jones called from the table.

Olivia passed the green peas.

Mr. Jones served the meatloaf. "What's gotten into that boy? He's never late to dinner."

A few minutes later, Herbie sat down at the table. His hair was slicked down with water and parted in the middle. "Sorry Mom, I had to brush my teeth."

"You brush *before* meals now?" Mr. Jones asked.

"Yup," Herbie said as he scooped some mashed potatoes onto his plate.

"He wants his breath to smell nice," Olivia said, "for Annabelle. Did you have fun at her house today?"

Herbie looked at Olivia and then blew some breath in her face.

"Hmm, wintergreen. Nice Erb."

"Glad you like it, *Olive!*" Herbie knew Olivia hated her nickname as much as he hated his. Erb reminded him of the hairy-looking seasonings people put on salads. Olivia hated the idea of being compared to a roly-poly olive.

"That's enough, you two," Mr. Jones scolded. "Are you going somewhere tonight, son?"

"To the library."

"What are you studying at the library?" Olivia was curious.

"Poetry," Herbie said. "Miss Pinkham told us we could do a poetry project together. She's even going to bind the pages we write into a book for the school library."

"Hmm." Olivia thought for a moment. "You might try looking up some poems by Carl Sandburg. He wrote a neat one called 'Fog.' We read it in English last week."

"Thanks, Olive. Carl who?"

"Sandburg. It rhymes with Hamburg."

"Got it!" Herbie stood up and dropped his napkin into his glass. "See you later. I told Annabelle I'd pick her up at six o'clock. Mr. Hodgekiss will give us a ride home."

"I sure don't get to see much of you," Mr. Jones said as Herbie ran to the door. Mr. Jones worked the night shift at an airplane factory so he slept during the day.

Annabelle was waiting on the front porch. She was petting her cat, Sukey. "Hi, Herbie," she said.

Herbie noticed she was wearing a pink ribbon in her hair and a pink blouse with a fuzzy white cat on the pocket.

As they walked to the library, Annabelle showed Herbie her new three-ring binder with 100 sheets of lined paper and the plastic pouch for all her pencils and erasers. "I got it for our poetry project."

Herbie held his green notebook in his arms. It was well worn now. "I think I'll just choose my best twelve poems for the book."

"Me too," Annabelle said. "I think that's a good idea."

"You do?" Herbie looked at Annabelle. He smelled her gardenia hair again.

"I do. And I'll include a table of contents page." Then Annabelle pointed out some daffodils along the way.

"Did you like the poem about daffodils by William Wordsworth?"

Herbie remembered it. "'Beside the lake, beneath the trees/Fluttering and dancing in the breeze,'" he recited.

"Gee, Herbie, I just showed you that poem this afternoon. You remembered all that?"

Herbie smiled as he looked into Annabelle's brown eyes. Then he walked into a fire hydrant and stumbled back. "That happens . . . sometimes," he mumbled.

As they neared the library on Wainwright Crescent, they passed Raymond's house. Ray was sitting on the porch petting Shadow.

"HEY, HERBIE!" he yelled, running down the steps.

"Oh, hi, Ray," Herbie replied, still thinking about Annabelle's eyes. He decided they reminded him of chocolate malt balls.

Annabelle didn't say anything. She didn't want to stand around and talk to Raymond. "We better move right along to the library, Herbie. Dad said I could only stay an hour."

"Library?" Ray repeated. "I'll come too."

Annabelle put her hands on her hips. "Herbie and I are doing a project, TOGETHER. Besides, I bet you don't even have a library card," Annabelle said holding up hers.

The boys noticed it was laminated.

Ray shrugged his shoulders. "So . . . I'll browse." He remembered his mom said that when she went shopping and had no money to spend.

Annabelle flared her nostrils and kept walking. "Come on, Herbie," she said.

As they walked up the steps to the library, they heard a tinkling noise behind them. It was Shadow's collar and license. Ray was pulling him along on a leash.

Annabelle ignored them. "What poet did you want to look up, Herbie?"

"Uh . . ." Herbie tried to remember who his sister had said. "Carl . . . Carl Hamburger."

Annabelle giggled as she pushed open the glass door. "I think you mean Carl Sandburg. Let's check in the card catalogue."

Herbie followed her gardenia scent.

Raymond, meanwhile, hurriedly tied Shadow to a parking meter in front of the library. Then he joined them at the card catalogue. "What'cha looking up?" he asked.

"Olivia told me some guy named Carl Sandburg writes good poetry. I want to read his poem 'Fog.'"

Ray watched Herbie's fingers pick their way through the cards. "Here it is!" Herbie wrote the number down.

"Shhh!" Annabelle whispered. She had already

selected a dozen books on poetry and was sitting at one of the long tables nearby. Several other people were studying. They looked like they were in high school. Herbie and Raymond walked over to where Annabelle was sitting.

"Sorry, Raymond," Annabelle said coldly, "there's just enough room for Herbie and me and our books. You can sit behind us at the next table."

Herbie was so excited about finding the 'Fog' poem that he didn't see the hurt look on Raymond's face.

Herbie read the poem aloud in a low voice. Ray peered over his shoulder from the next table.

FOG
by Carl Sandburg

The fog comes
on little cat feet.

It sits looking
over harbor and city
on silent haunches
and then moves on.

"Gee, it doesn't rhyme," Herbie said.

"It must not be a real poem," Ray replied.

"No . . . it has to be a poem. Olivia said he's a poet."

Annabelle looked over from her book. "I like poems that rhyme better."

"What does *haunches* mean?" Herbie asked.

Annabelle was disappointed that she didn't know. "I'll get the big Webster dictionary, and we can look it up."

When she returned they flipped through the pages until they came to the *H* section.

"Here it is." Annabelle pointed at the word with her pink fingernail. "It says 'the two rounded parts of your lower back.'"

"Rounded parts?" Herbie was still confused.

Raymond leaned back on his chair. "They mean rear end."

Herbie was impressed with Raymond's quickness.

Annabelle giggled. Then she whispered, "My mom always told me to call it derrière, that's the French word for it."

"Derrière?" Herbie said. "We call them buns, at my house."

Raymond cracked up.

Annabelle snickered.

When the librarian looked over, Annabelle's face turned red. "Shhh! We're going to get in trouble."

Raymond was disappointed they had to stop. It was the first time he had seen Annabelle silly.

Herbie went back to reading.

When Annabelle looked up again to see if the librarian was still staring at them, she noticed something black and hairy underneath the card catalogue. It had four legs.

"Shadow!" she blurted out. Then she quickly covered her mouth with her hands. She was being noisy again.

"Huh?" Herbie looked up.

"What?" Ray turned around.

Annabelle lowered her voice. "Over by the card catalogue."

"Where?"

"Underneath."

"Oh, no!" Ray said. "When he sits on his . . ."

"Haunches . . ." Herbie and Annabelle said together.

". . . that means he has to . . ."

Raymond shot out of his seat, grabbed Shadow's leash, and pulled him to the door. He was glad the librarian had left her desk.

As soon as they were outside, Shadow ran to a big bush.

Boy, that was close! Ray thought.

Ray sat down on the library steps and waited for his dog. When Shadow returned, he sniffed at Ray's armpit.

Ray put his arm around Shadow and scratched his neck. "I'm glad I have you, ol' boy!"

Then he peered sadly through the glass door. He saw Herbie and Annabelle laughing. Herbie didn't even care that he was gone. They sure don't need me, he thought.

Ray wanted to cry, but he didn't. He hugged Shadow instead. What was the matter with Herbie, anyway? Was he sick or something?

Then Ray noticed they had stopped laughing.

Herbie's green notebook slipped off the table and fell on the floor. When both of them stooped down to get it, their heads bumped.

Annabelle blushed.

Herbie was only inches from Annabelle's eyes. He just stared into them and didn't move.

Ray jumped up! Oh no, he thought. Ray knew what was wrong with Herbie. He was sick all right. Lovesick. Herbie Jones liked a girl. Herbie Jones had the girl disease, the G Disease!

Ray couldn't desert his buddy now. He had to keep a closer watch on things, and just maybe there was time to save him before it was too late.

5

It All Happened
at the Fish Grotto

Clinkity, clinkity.

Saturday morning, Herbie shook the last penny out of his baseball bank. $2.61. His life savings.

Herbie stuffed the 261 pennies into his side pockets and rattled into the kitchen for breakfast.

"Morning, Herb," Olivia said as she poured two glasses of orange juice. "Did you like Carl Sandburg?"

Herbie sat down. "I sure did! I even wrote my first poem that doesn't rhyme because of him. Want to hear it?"

Olivia nodded. Her mouth was full of cereal.

Herbie laid his green notebook on the table and began reading aloud.

A daddy longlegs
comes across the sealing.
It sits looking
over the bedroom
on its hanches
and then walks on.

"I *love* it!" Olivia exclaimed. "Make sure you use
that one for your poetry project."

"Thanks." Herbie looked forward to showing it
to Annabelle.

When the phone rang, Herbie picked it up.

"Hi, Ray, how are you?" he said.

"I'm okay. How are YOU?"

"Fine. What's up?"

"Are we going fishing as usual? It's Saturday
morning."

"Oh . . . I'm sorry, Ray. I can't."

"Why not?"

"Because Annabelle and me . . ."

"Annabelle and *I*," Olivia interrupted.

Herbie shook his fist at his sister. He hated it
when she corrected him. "We're going to the li-

57

brary to finish our project. Her parents are driving us to some restaurant for lunch. Probably Burger Paradise."

Ray had half suspected Herbie was going to see Annabelle. "Where are you getting the money? You might have to pay for your own meal."

Herbie was quiet for a moment. Then he answered, "My baseball bank."

"THAT'S YOUR LIFE SAVINGS FOR WORMS!"

Herbie shrugged. "I'm using it. It's mine, okay?"

"You're gonna blow your life savings—your worm money—all on lunch with her and her parents?"

"Uh huh." Somehow, as Herbie heard Ray's words, the idea didn't seem that great anymore. "I have to go now, Ray. I told her I'd meet her at the library."

"Good luck," Ray said, hanging up. He immediately went to his hall closet. He had to patrol the situation. But first, he needed a foolproof disguise.

His dad's old black overcoat. Perfect!

Ray put it on. As he flipped up the collar, he walked to the library feeling like a detective, even if the bottom two feet of his coat were dragging.

Ray hid in the bushes near the library door and waited.

Herbie and Annabelle worked all morning at the table next to the poster that had an owl on it. It said, "Wise Guys Read!"

At eleven-forty-five, Herbie scooted his chair closer to Annabelle's. He wanted to show her his daddy-longlegs poem and see what she thought.

Herbie watched as she read it. He noticed she still smelled nice.

"We can't use it," she said coldly.

"Why not?" Herbie was hurt.

"It doesn't rhyme."

"A poem doesn't have to."

"I know that, Herbie, but I want to use poems that rhyme for our project."

Herbie didn't like the way Annabelle said "I." He had thought they were doing the project together.

Herbie stood up. He was getting restless and hungry. "We better start looking for your parents. They said they'd be here at noon."

When the Hodgekiss car pulled up in front of the library, Ray recognized it right away. It had HODGE written on the license plate. He watched as Herbie and Annabelle came out of the library.

When Herbie got in the car, he moved his hand across the blue velvet upholstery. Nice, he thought. Much nicer than his and definitely nicer than Ray's. Shadow had chewed half of Ray's backseat off, and the stuffing was coming out.

Herbie leaned back and looked out the window. He felt like a big wheel as they drove down the street.

Hey! he thought to himself. They just passed Burger Paradise! Mr. Hodgekiss was pulling into a parking lot down the street. The one next to the Fish Grotto.

"We're going there?" Herbie asked Annabelle. She nodded.

Herbie felt his pockets. He wondered if he would have enough money. This was a rich place.

As they walked into the lobby, Herbie saw a bubbling fountain half covered with fishing nets and cork weights. It looked like a wishing well.

"Want to buy a wish for a penny?" Annabelle asked.

Herbie shook his head. He couldn't afford it. He might need every penny to pay for his meal.

A lady with a lacy blouse and a black skirt asked how many were in their party.

Mr. Hodgekiss said four.

Herbie wondered why the lady said "party." They weren't even wearing funny hats.

They followed the lady to a booth next to a window and a picture of a sea captain. She handed them a menu with a ship on it.

Herbie opened his up and looked for the cheapest meal.

Annabelle knew right away what she wanted.

"I think I'll have the Catch of the Day. Halibut."

"Me too," said Mrs. Hodgekiss.

"How about you, Herbie?" Mr. Hodgekiss asked.

"Eh . . . eh . . ." Herbie stammered. He

couldn't find anything for around $2.00.

"I'm treating, you know," Mr. Hodgekiss said.

"You are?" Boy, was Herbie happy about that. "Well, then I think I'll have that hamburger and french fries plate."

Annabelle made a face. "You don't order hamburger at a fish restaurant."

"How come it's on the menu then?"

"Look where it is," she pointed.

Herbie did and blushed. It was under the Kiddy Specials.

"Why don't you just order what we are," Annabelle suggested, "the Catch of the Day."

"Okay, I'll have the habit too."

"Halibut," Annabelle corrected.

Herbie studied Annabelle. She was beginning to remind him of his sister.

Ten minutes later, when the meals arrived, Herbie looked at his. The thin pieces of fish had a nice golden crust on them. He started to eat some.

"Your napkin . . ." Annabelle whispered.

Herbie put the napkin on his lap.

"Lemon?" Mrs. Hodgekiss offered.

"Thank you." Herbie took a slice off the plate and began squeezing it over his fish. As he did, the lemon slipped out of his hand and shot into the air.

Mr. and Mrs. Hodgekiss watched the lemon fly into the picture of the sea captain and then fall to the floor.

Annabelle gasped.

Mrs. Hodgekiss raised her eyebrows.

Mr. Hodgekiss smiled. "That's okay, Herbie. The poor guy up there spends all his time watching all this food. Now he finally gets to taste some."

Herbie chuckled. He liked Mr. Hodgekiss.

As Herbie ate his fish, he noticed something lodged in the crust. It was a hair. A stubborn one too. He tried to pull it out with his fingers, but when he did the piece of fish dangled and swung back and forth like a yo-yo.

Mrs. Hodgekiss put her fork down.

Mr. Hodgekiss did too.

Annabelle covered her mouth with her napkin.

Herbie decided to use his tweezers. He took them out of his back pocket and carefully began the operation. First he took his fork in his left hand

and held the fish still. Then he used his right hand to tweeze the hair out of the crust.

Perfect.

The hair slid slowly out.

Mrs. Hodgekiss put her hand over her heart. Annabelle cringed.

Herbie was surprised they were watching. As he held up the hair to the light, he said, "It's a white one."

Annabelle complained, "I'm never eating here again as long as I live."

"I'll take care of this," Mr. Hodgekiss said, standing up. "I'm going to speak with the manager. I didn't know hair was on the menu."

"Good," Mrs. Hodgekiss said. "We'll meet you in the lobby, dear."

Herbie followed Annabelle and her mother. When they got to the wishing well in the lobby, Annabelle stopped. "What is making all that noise, Herbie?"

"Oh, that's just my pennies."

"Pennies?" Annabelle looked at his bulging

pockets. "Why, Herbie Jones, you wanted to treat me to some wishes all along."

Mrs. Hodgekiss smiled and excused herself to the ladies room.

Herbie looked into the wishing well. He didn't know what to say.

"How many pennies did you bring?"

"Uh . . . two . . ." Herbie stammered.

"Two?"

". . . two hundred or so."

"Oh, Herbie! What a wonderful surprise!" And then Annabelle closed her eyes and waited. "I'll start wishing just as soon as you put them in."

Them? Herbie thought. He dropped four pennies into the water.

Annabelle opened up one eye. "All of them."

"All of them?" Herbie squeaked.

"Just think . . . two hundred wishes for me."

Herbie gritted his teeth. This money was supposed to be for worms. Reluctantly, he emptied his pockets. Goodbye, worms. Hello, Annabelle.

He didn't think much of the trade.

6

Herbie in the Soup

On Monday morning Ray was waiting at the corner in front of Mrs. Von Whistle's garden. When he saw Herbie he asked, "So, you didn't go to Burger Paradise after all."

Herbie looked surprised. "How did you know?"

"I've got my ways." Ray was pleased that his overcoat disguise had turned out to be foolproof. It didn't bother him that a lot of people had looked at him kind of funny when he walked through Burger Paradise.

"Well, you were right, Ray. I wasted good worm money. It wasn't any fun at all."

"Sure, Herbie, sure." Ray remembered how

Herbie looked when he got into the Hodgekiss car. Like a big shot. "You liked it all right, you've got a bad case of the G Disease."

Herbie stopped walking. "G Disease? What's that?"

Ray pointed to Herbie's face. "You like a girl. G-R-I-L," he spelled. "And that g-r-i-l is Annabelle Louisa Hodgekiss. You've liked her ever since you danced with her Friday."

Herbie dropped his lunch in the garden and took a step towards Ray. "Have not!"

"Have too!" Ray replied.

The boys were nose to nose now.

"I liked her ONE DAY ONLY!" Herbie shouted. "Just Friday, okay?"

Ray stepped back. "You liked Annabelle Louisa Hodgekiss one day only?"

"Well . . . maybe a day and a half."

Ray beamed. Herbie's case of the G Disease didn't last as long as the chicken pox. It didn't leave any marks either.

"Most of Saturday," Herbie continued, "I was either bugged or bored. Do you know what it's like to copy poems all afternoon and worry about dropping cookie crumbs on the floor?"

Ray shook his head. "Forget it. It's over."

"Yeah? I know it. You know it. But does *she* know it? That's the big question."

Ray looked worried.

"I'll find out soon enough," Herbie replied. "We better get going. It's late."

Ray bent down and picked a handful of flowers from Mrs. Von Whistle's garden.

"Hey, what are you doing?" Herbie asked.

"If we're late, I may have some buttering up to do. I'm not staying after school."

"You're giving Miss Pinkham dandelions?"

Ray looked at the flowers. "Is that what these things are? I thought they were daisies."

Herbie shook his head and then hurried up the street, kicking a rock.

When the boys got to the school lawn, no one was around. That meant the first bell had rung. They wondered if the late bell had rung too.

The boys darted down the hall and stopped at

the classroom door. Miss Pinkham had her back to the class. She was writing the word SOUP on the blackboard.

Both of them tiptoed to their seats and sat down quietly. Ray stuffed his flowers in his desk. He figured he didn't need them now. As soon as Herbie sat down, he remembered he'd forgotten something. His homework. It was in his lunch bag, and his lunch bag was . . .

"You're five minutes late," a voice whispered.

Herbie turned his head. It was Annabelle. She was the reason he had dropped his lunch in Mrs. Von Whistle's garden, and now she was the reason he didn't have his homework!

Herbie glanced outside the window at the maple tree. He didn't feel like looking at Annabelle.

"I brought something for you," she whispered.

Herbie rolled his eyeballs. He had a feeling he'd better be very careful today.

"It's in your desk," she continued.

Slowly Herbie reached inside and pulled out a cellophane package. It looked like long, dried, greenish-brown leaves.

71

"It's real good for you because it contains iodine," Annabelle added.

Iodine? Herbie remembered that stuff. His mom put it on his cuts and scratches to kill germs.

"Do you know what it is?" Annabelle smiled.

"Of course I do." Herbie stuck out his tongue. "It's poison."

"Don't be silly, Herbie Jones. Iodine in food is a trace mineral that is good for us. It's essential for our thyroid gland, and our thyroid gland regulates our growth."

Herbie waited a moment to see if Annabelle's health lecture was over.

It was.

"So, what is this stuff, anyway?" he asked.

"Seaweed."

"Seaweed?"

"Yes. Enjoy it with your lunch."

"Thanks." Herbie figured that was all he was going to get for his lunch.

Miss Pinkham rested a piece of chalk on her ear, and then turned to the class. "Boys and girls, you know that we have been studying nutrition, and that today we planned to make our own vegetable soup. For homework, you were to bring in an ingredient for the soup."

Ray frowned. He'd forgotten.

"I've borrowed a large pot from the cafeteria and brought my hot plate from home. Just be careful when you come up not to touch the pot. It's hot."

Miss Pinkham took out her black grade book and began calling names. "John Greenweed," she said.

Everyone watched as John carried a big sack to the front of the room. "These are from my aunt's garden, Louise Von Whistle." He dumped six tomatoes into the pot. Some of the broth spurted into the air. A drop landed on Miss Pinkham's nose.

"Please use the ladle, boys and girls, when you are putting a vegetable in," she said as she marked a point in her book for John and then wiped the broth off her face.

Ray sat back confidently. He had an idea.

"Phillip McDoogle?" Miss Pinkham called.

Herbie began to squirm in his seat. What was

he going to do when his turn came? He knew that Phillip had lucked out. His mom always packed him a carrot in his lunch.

"Annabelle Louisa Hodgekiss," Miss Pinkham continued.

Annabelle resnapped her rainbow barrette and walked over to the pot. "I brought rosemary."

Ray clapped his hands. "She's putting a girl in the soup!"

The boys laughed.

Annabelle flared her nostrils. "Most people know that rosemary is an herb."

Herbie sat up. Erb? That reminded him of the awful nickname his sister used. He watched Annabelle sprinkle the hairy-looking things into the soup.

Ray shook his head. "I guess I was wrong about Annabelle putting a girl in the soup. She's putting Herb Jones in it instead!"

Everyone laughed this time, except Herbie. He shot a dirty look at his buddy and held up his fist.

Miss Pinkham put her hands on her hips. "Since you're so concerned, Raymond Martin, about what's going in our soup, perhaps *you* would like to be next?" Then she looked at the six zeroes after Raymond's name. "Or did you forget your homework again?"

Ray popped right out of his seat. He was ready! "Miss Pinkham, I want you to know that from now on I'm doing my homework."

"Oh?" Miss Pinkham raised her eyebrows. "And what did you bring for our soup?"

Ray held something behind his back. "Something I picked fresh from the garden just this morning. My uncle says it makes good wine."

The class was half off their seats waiting to see what he had.

"Dandelions!" Ray grinned as he dangled them over the soup.

The class gasped.

Miss Pinkham's eyes widened as she watched three ants crawl into a yellow flower. "Why don't you put them in that vase over there on my desk," she suggested. "We'll appreciate them with . . . our eyes."

Ray shrugged his shoulders. "If you say so, but

do I still get a homework point? I brought something in from Mrs. Von Whistle's garden too."

John Greenweed shot a look at Ray.

Miss Pinkham, who seemed in a fog, marked a
point for Ray and then looked down the list of
names. "Ah . . . I think Herbie Jones is next."

Herbie was thinking about the potato he had
packed in his lunch bag, which he didn't have with
him.

"Herbie?" Miss Pinkham repeated.

Quickly Herbie looked around. There was noth-
ing else. Herbie was in a desperate situation and
he had to use it. Slowly, he reached into his desk.
Very slowly he walked to the front of the room
with Annabelle's gift.

"Hmm, that looks interesting, Herbie. What is
it?" Miss Pinkham asked.

Herbie handed her the package. "Seaweed."

"*Seaweed?*" Miss Pinkham's head jerked. The
chalk slipped off her ear and broke into little pieces
on the floor.

"Yes, Miss Pinkham. Seaweed has trace ele-
ments of iodine in it. Iodine is important for the
tie-rod clam. And everybody knows the tie-rod

clam is an important part of our body."

Annabelle giggled.

Miss Pinkham smiled. "I think you are referring to the thyroid gland; and you're right, Herbie, it is important. But where did you get the seaweed?"

Herbie, stopped cold. "Wh . . . where?" He looked at the class, then at Miss Pinkham. He didn't want them to know he had gotten a gift from a girl. Especially Annabelle. Not now!

"Uh . . ." Herbie continued, "this seaweed came from the ah . . . ocean. Yes, the ocean!" Herbie was pleased he had come up with a good answer.

"Really?" Miss Pinkham replied. "You mean the ocean is drying and packaging its own seaweed now in these cellophane wrappers?"

The class laughed.

Annabelle raised her hand. "I got it from the health food store downtown, Miss Pinkham," Annabelle offered.

Everyone stared at Annabelle. She seemed to enjoy the sudden attention. Then they looked back at Herbie. His face was red.

"Well," Miss Pinkham said, "it certainly is an interesting ingredient." The class watched as she tore open the package and let the dried leaves tumble into the soup.

As Herbie walked back to his seat, Phillip snickered, "Ooo . . . gotta present from your girlfriend?"

"Girlfriend?" Herbie glared at Phil.

"Shhh!" Annabelle put her finger to her lips. "We don't want everybody to know."

"Know? Know what?" Herbie said as he plopped down in his chair. "That I like seaweed?"

"You know what, Herbie Jones." Annabelle twirled some hair around her fingers. And then she did something else. She shot Herbie a little wink.

Herbie's eyes bulged.

That was it. Things had gone too far. Now not only Annabelle, but the whole class, thought she was his girlfriend. He had to do something about the mess he was in.

But what?

Until the three o'clock bell, Herbie fixed his eyes on the pot. He was in the soup. Why not look at it.

7

Dad to the Rescue

When Herbie got home, Olivia was in front of the TV set doing her homework.

"I need your help, Olivia," he said.

"Not now, I'm watching *General Infirmary*."

Herbie was disappointed. Olivia was a big help, sometimes. She wasn't any now.

"Mom home yet?"

"Shhh! You know when she gets home. At five o'clock."

"Dad up?"

"He's in the kitchen. I'm watching this, Erb. Don't bother me."

Mr. Jones was pouring some milk in his coffee cup and opening the day's mail.

"Hi, Dad," Herbie said, holding out an empty glass.

His dad filled it with the remaining milk in the carton. "Guess we'll have to buy some more tonight."

Herbie didn't say anything. He had never talked to his dad about a girl problem before. But he had to talk to somebody. He couldn't wait until five o'clock when his mom got home from Dipping Donuts.

"I got a problem, Dad," he said.

"Oh?" Mr. Jones looked up from a letter he was reading. "Bad grade on a spelling test?"

Herbie shook his head. "Worse. Some girl at school thinks I like her as a girlfriend. But I don't."

"Hmm," Mr. Jones sipped some coffee. "Well, whenever something like that happened to me . . ."

"It happened to *you*, Dad?"

"Couple of times."

"Really?"

"Hey, I wasn't always this ugly," he joked. "When it happened to me, I made it a point to be straightforward and honest about it. You know, businesslike."

"Businesslike?" Herbie was curious.

"Talk the way business people do. You get it done and it's over with, but you do it in a polite way. Not nasty."

"Hmm," Herbie muttered.

"For example," Mr. Jones continued, as he held up the morning's mail, "I got this reply to an application I sent in for a day job. They didn't want me but they said it in a nice way. You see, Herbie, when you work in a business world, you learn how to do things like that."

"Do you need this letter?" Herbie asked.

"No, you keep it. I was just going to toss it in the garbage. Someday, Herbie, I'm going to be in that business world. I'm tired of working night shifts."

Herbie got up from his chair and went over to his dad. "Thanks, Dad, I think you just saved my life."

"Well, that makes my day, Herbie. Hearing something like that. I just wish I could be around more often."

For some reason Herbie got the urge to hug his dad. And he did. It was the bear hug kind. Long and strong.

Herbie was ready to straighten out the girlfriend mess he had gotten himself into. He was going to tell Annabelle how he felt. In a businesslike way.

First, though, he had to check with Olivia about something. "Can I use your typewriter for ten minutes?" he asked.

"Don't bother me now. Oglethorpe is just finding out about his inheritance."

"Can I?" Herbie pestered.

"YES!"

Herbie had to ask about one more thing. "What do businessmen wear?" He didn't know. His dad went to work in a factory, not an office.

"Look at Oglethorpe, he's a businessman," Olivia said, pointing to a man with silver hair on the TV screen.

Got it, Herbie thought. And then he went upstairs to do some important typing and make a trip to the attic.

8

Getting Down to Business

The next morning Herbie walked to the corner. Ray was surprised to see Herbie dressed in a white shirt and tie, carrying a briefcase.

"Where did you get that thing?" Ray asked.

"It belonged to my granddad. I found it in the attic. Like my tie?"

"You transferring to a Catholic school or something?"

"No, I just have some important business to take care of."

"What's that mean?"

And then Herbie filled Ray in on all the details.

When Herbie entered the classroom, Miss Pinkham spoke to him right away. "You look so nice, Herbie. I'm sorry it's not a square-dancing day."

Herbie smiled and then walked directly to his seat, stopping briefly by Annabelle's.

"Good morning, Miss Hodgekiss," he said. "I have a letter for you." And he dropped it on her desk.

Annabelle sat up, looked at Herbie twice, and then opened up the letter. She read it to herself:

dear Miss Hodgekiss,

    thank you for your interest in the position
of girlfriend to Herbie Jones .
    So many qaulified people have applied that
it has made selecting just one a diffficult task.
    i have chosen Someone who more nearly meats
my imediate needs.
    However, be assured that your application
will be kept on file inthe event another opening
should come up.
    Thank you for your intrest in Herbie Jones.

                 sincerly,

            Herbert D. Jones

            Herbert D. Jones

Herbie watched from the corner of his eye. He

wondered if she was going to put her head down, or break out in tears, or do what she did when she really got angry—write his name on her ALH memo pad with three checks after it.

Annabelle didn't do any of that.

She just stared at Herbie.

All morning long.

Maybe it was his striped tie. Maybe it was the crisp white shirt or the briefcase, but Annabelle was more attentive than ever.

At noontime when the bell rang to line up for lunch, Annabelle stood right behind Herbie.

"More than anything," she said to him, "I love a challenge, especially a businesslike challenge. So if *I'm* not your girlfriend, who is? I'd like to know my competition, Herbert D."

Herbie looked at Raymond. Ray shrugged his shoulders. He wasn't much help lately, Herbie thought.

"My girlfriend?" Herbie asked.

"Yes, Herbert, the one you selected out of all those qualified people."

"Uh . . ." Herbie started to stammer. He

loosened his tie and unbuttoned his top button. He was losing his business cool.

"Yes?" Annabelle waited for the name.

"Uh, she has a regular name. Real regular."

"Really? What is it?"

Herbie stepped forward in the cafeteria line. Desperately he looked around for an idea. When he spotted Mrs. Coffey seasoning the cole slaw, he thought of something. "Uh . . . Pepper. Her name is Pepper."

Annabelle raised her eyebrows. "Pepper? That's not a very regular name. There's no Pepper in our class, and I bet there's not one girl named Pepper at Laurel Woods Elementary School."

"She doesn't go here," Herbie said, grabbing a tray. He didn't want to hang around for any more questions. He wished Ray would hurry up. Why did he always have to ask for two desserts?

Annabelle took two napkins. She had a feeling Herbie wasn't telling the truth, and she wasn't going to let him get away with it. "Pepper who?" she quizzed. "Don't you even know your girl-friend's last name?"

Now what was he going to say? Herbie stared at the pizza on his plate. Then he looked at the sausage topping. Slowly a smile appeared on Herbie's face. "Sure I do," he said. "Pepper . . . Roni."

9

To Cheat or Not to Cheat

As Herbie and Ray carried their trays of pizza out of the lunch line, John Greenweed and Phillip McDoogle motioned to them.

"We got two seats saved over here," John shouted.

Good, Herbie thought. At least he didn't have to sit at the same table as Annabelle. She might ask him questions about Pepper Roni.

"How come the white shirt and tie?" Phillip asked.

"Huh?"

John grinned. "Want to impress your girlfriend, Annabelle?"

Herbie remembered what his dad said about

being straightforward and honest. He didn't have to type any letter for John and Phillip. He would just tell them the way it was. "Listen, you guys, Annabelle is NOT my girlfriend, so stop talking about it."

"Fine. How come the shirt and the tie?" Phillip asked again.

"I had some private business to take care of."

"We believe you," John replied.

Herbie was glad. But somehow he didn't think Annabelle understood. Being businesslike with her had backfired. She liked him even more now.

"So let's get to the meat of this conversation," John urged.

"Yeah," Ray said, popping a meatball into his mouth.

"Not food, Ray," John corrected. "A discovery. The discovery of the century. Tell 'em about it, Phil."

Phil finished chewing some garlic bread and began. "You know what tomorrow is . . ."

Both Herbie and Ray shrugged their shoulders. Their mouths were too full to talk.

"The spelling bee between the girls and the boys."

Herbie and Ray had forgotten about it. There was so much other business going on.

"You didn't forget how the girls creamed us the last time? We MUST get revenge."

Herbie chomped into some celery.

Ray wiped his mouth on his sleeve.

"So," Phillip continued, "the good news is that I have found the word list for the spelling bee."

"YOU WHAT?" Herbie and Ray blurted out.

Phillip lowered his voice. "Right next to Miss Pinkham's red porcupine pencil holder. I saw it when I walked by her desk this morning."

"Isn't that a discovery?" John said as he fiddled with his empty asthma inhalator.

"Now all we have to do is go up to the teacher's desk and look at the words. Ray could look at the first five, Phillip could take the second five, me the next five, and Herbie the last five. There were only twenty words on the list."

"But that's cheating," Herbie said.

"So. Our honor is at stake, boys. If we lose another spelling bee to the girls we're doomed. And the only way we can beat them is by cheating."

"You're going to cheat for honor?" Herbie asked.

"Yes," Phil said.

Ray joined the conversation. "I was the first person to sit down in the last bee. I misspelled a tricky word."

"I remember that," John said. "You couldn't spell *is*."

Phil and John laughed.

"Funny," Ray replied, "but I'll tell you something. I can spell sounds just fine. *Is* sounds like *i-z*. There should be a *z* at the end, not an *s*."

"*Is* does sound a lot like *i-z*," Herbie agreed.

"Well anyway," John said, "the question is are we going to cheat or not?"

"Cheat!" said Phillip.

"Sounds fine to me," Ray said. "I'm tired of being the first one to sit down."

"I'm in then," John added, "so it's up to you, Herbie."

"I think we should try to beat the girls fair and square."

"Sure, sure, Herbie, and WHO is going to spell better than Annabelle? She can spell ANY-THING!"

"So can I," said Herbie. "A-n-y-t-h-i-n-g."

"Funny. You know what I mean. Annabelle wins everything."

And when Phillip said that, Raymond had a powerful idea. "Just a minute, guys, I gotta have a word with Herbie."

Ray pulled Herbie over to the drinking fountain. "Look, Herbie, this is the perfect way to get out of your girlfriend mess. If we win the spelling bee, Annabelle will hate the boys for beating her. That includes you! We'll get the silent treatment."

Herbie thought about it. It was true. Annabelle wasn't a good sport. He remembered how she treated people who didn't vote for her daisy poster.

It would make things a lot easier. But was it right?

No, it wasn't right, Herbie thought.

94

Then his eye caught Annabelle's and she waved.
And then she did something else.

She winked again.

That's it, Herbie said to himself when he returned with Ray to the table. "Count me in."

Shortly after math started, Ray got out of his seat and walked over to Miss Pinkham's desk. He asked a question about fractions, and then while she was explaining, he looked at the first five words on the list:

1. pen
2. light bulb
3. flour
4. paper
5. apples

Phillip asked for help after Raymond.
Then John did.
And then Herbie.

. ——— .

The boys met at John's house right after school.

"Okay, you guys," John said after he passed around a can of cheese balls. "Let's compare words."

Raymond started, since he had been the first one up at the teacher's desk. "There was pen, light bulb, flour . . ."

"Which flour? The kind you put in a vase, or on chicken?" John quizzed.

Raymond hesitated. "The kind you put in a vase: f-l-o-u-r."

John wrote it down neatly on his portable blackboard.

Phil looked at his scribbled notes. "Produce, coffee, sugar, and, I think, cremate."

"My great grandmother was cremated," John reflected.

"So were we in the last spelling bee by the girls," Phillip mumbled.

No one laughed.

"Unusual word—cremate," John said.

"How about the next one: cat litter. Who would think that would be on a spelling list?"

"Tricky," Ray replied.

"One or two *t*'s?" John asked.

"Two," Phillip answered.

The session continued for twenty minutes. Herbie remained quiet for most of the time. He just felt uncomfortable.

At midnight that night, Raymond's phone rang. He picked it up on the second ring because the phone was by the couch where he was sleeping. For the last week Ray had been sleeping downstairs in the living room because it was too hot on the second floor.

"Hello?" he said in a sleepy voice.

Herbie thought he should use code language. This call was top secret. "992, this is Double 030," he said, trying to cup his hand over the phone. He didn't want to wake up his sister or mother.

"Why are you calling so late?" Ray yawned.

"I can't sleep."

Ray sat up on the couch. "Great. I was sleeping just fine until you called. What's the matter?"

"Plenty. We can't go through with that spelling

97

bee tomorrow. It's not right, Raymond. And we could get in a lot of trouble."

"No one is going to find out," Ray replied. "Besides, you said yourself, it's the best way for you to stop this girlfriend stuff."

"I have a better plan."

"What?"

"Let's take on the girls fair and square. I think we have a good chance."

"You're a dreamer, Herbie. And speaking of dreams, I was having a good one. Good night."

"Just a minute, Ray!"

"What?"

"What if your mom found out about our cheating?"

Ray took a deep swallow. "She'd use that old Ping-Pong paddle with the rubber off one side."

"Yeah," Herbie continued, "and you know which side she'd use on your . . . haunches!"

Ray smiled even though he was sleepy. He liked that word too. "I'll think about it," Ray said.

"That's what I've been doing, and my conscience bothers me."

"Night, Herbie." Ray clicked the phone.

At three o'clock in the morning, Herbie's phone rang. Herbie picked it up on the fourth ring. He was still half asleep, but he had a good idea who it was.

"Ray?" he said.

"Yeah, it's me. My conscience is bothering me."

"Good. Then you'll confess with me tomorrow?"

"Yeah."

"Night, Ray."

"Night, Herbie."

10

The Spelling Bee

Herbie and Ray talked with John and Phillip under the maple tree at school.

"Well," Phillip complained, "I think we're throwing a perfectly good plan down a rat hole."

"Yeah, we'll be washing the blackboard all week," John argued, "and we'll get stomped today in the spelling bee."

"We gotta do this, guys."

Ray, John and Phillip all looked at Herbie. Then they followed him into the classroom.

Miss Pinkham greeted them at the door. Herbie started the confession about the spelling list. Miss Pinkham listened attentively. She looked like she was going to laugh, but she didn't.

"Well, boys, that so-called spelling list wouldn't have helped you at all."

"It wouldn't have?" Phillip asked.

"No. It was my grocery list."

"GROCERY LIST!" the boys shouted.

Phillip rolled his eyeballs.

John hit his forehead with his fist. "But, you had cremate on that list, Miss Pinkham. How could that be?"

Miss Pinkham tried to picture the grocery list in her mind. "Cremate? Hmm." And then she started to laugh. "That was Cremora. I use it in my coffee."

"Oh!" John hit his forehead again.

"You certainly did the right thing to tell me about it, boys. There will be no punishment."

John looked up. "No punishment?"

"No."

"We have Herbie to thank for that, Miss Pinkham," John admitted. "It was his idea to tell you."

The entire class turned pin quiet.

Miss Pinkham walked over to Herbie. "Is that true?" she asked.

Herbie looked at the nails in the wooden floor.

Ray was so happy the way it had turned out that he answered for him. "It sure is, Miss Pinkham. Herbie had to talk us into it."

Miss Pinkham patted Herbie on the back. Then the entire class applauded. Especially Annabelle.

When Herbie looked up, he saw her beaming at him. Oh no, he thought. Now she thinks I'm some kind of hero. She'll never give up on this girlfriend business.

Unless . . . unless the boys could pull off a miracle and win the spelling bee.

Miss Pinkham clapped her hands twice. "Boys and girls, when I ring this bell, we will begin our spelling bee."

Annabelle looked over at Herbie one last time and smiled.

Herbie immediately turned to Ray and John and Phillip. "We gotta give this spelling bee our best shot, guys. I think we can do it. We *have* to."

Raymond liked the positive sound of Herbie's voice. So did John and Phillip.

Miss Pinkham lined the boys up by the black-board and the girls by the windows. Ray felt a surge of energy.

Herbie stood tall.

John put his inhalator in his pocket and crossed his fingers.

Phillip put his hands behind his back.

Finally, Miss Pinkham rang her blue ceramic bell. "Okay, boys and girls, we will begin. Remember, there is no talking. And, you MUST spell the word correctly the first time."

Miss Pinkham told the class the first word would go to Raymond Martin since he was at the front of the boys' line.

The girls beamed. Margie Sherman whispered something to Annabelle.

"Raymond," Miss Pinkham said, "your first word is . . ."

Herbie nodded as if to say, you can do it, Raymond.

". . . *hamburger*," Miss Pinkham pronounced.

Ray smiled at Herbie. He knew that word easy. He had seen it lots of times at Burger Paradise.

"H-a-m-b-u-r-g-e-r," Raymond spelled.

"Correct," Miss Pinkham said.

All the boys cheered and clapped, especially Raymond.

"Now, now . . . There will be no cheering *during* the spelling bee."

When the boys stopped, Ray asked, "Do you want me to spell fries or shake?"

Miss Pinkham smiled. "No, Raymond. *I* give the words. Not you. Now, *no* more talking."

The children were silent.

"Margie," Miss Pinkham continued, "your word is *germ.*"

Margie stepped forward. "Germ, j-e-r-m."

"I'm sorry, that's incorrect. You'll have to sit down."

The boys wanted to clap, but they didn't dare. It was especially hard for Raymond to keep quiet. This was the first spelling bee in which he hadn't sat down before everyone else.

"Herbie Jones, spell *pound.*"

Herbie remembered that word. He had gotten it right before on a spelling test. "P-o-u-n-d."

"Correct. Now, Annabelle Louisa Hodgekiss."

Annabelle stepped forward with confidence.

"*Square*," Miss Pinkham said.

"S-q-u-a-r-e." Annabelle spelled it easily.

"John Greenweed," Miss Pinkham continued, "*locomotive*."

"L-o-c-o-m-o-t-i-v-e."

"Correct."

The spelling bee continued back and forth for ten minutes. Ray sat down in the second round. He spelled *said*, s-e-d. Most of the children were out by the fifth round.

Only five remained standing now. Three boys and two girls.

"Phillip," Miss Pinkham asked, "spell *tweezers*."

The class was pin quiet. They knew it was a tough word. Herbie wished it was his turn. He knew that word by heart. It was written on his Trusty Tweezers that he kept in his back pocket.

Phillip began to stammer. "T-w-e-z-e-r-s."

"I'm sorry, that's incorrect."

The girls tried not to make any noise, but they were excited that the sides were even now.

"Sarah Sitwellington, the word goes to you. *Tweezers.*"

Sarah slowly stepped forward. "Tweezers," she repeated the word, "t-w-e-e-z-i-r-s."

"Incorrect, Sarah."

It was John Greenweed's turn. He started to wheeze. His breathing was uneasy.

"Should you go to the nurse for some medication?" Miss Pinkham asked.

"No . . . I'm . . . okay. Uh, tweezers . . . t-w-e-z-o-r-s."

"Incorrect, you'll have to sit down."

"I think I'm wheezing," John said.

"Then please go to the nurse," Miss Pinkham directed gently.

Herbie and Annabelle were left.

The class didn't move.

Annabelle knew it was her turn. Suddenly her mood changed. She glared at Herbie. She also seemed uneasy.

Herbie couldn't wait to spell it. He even managed a smile, which made Annabelle frown.

106

"Your word is the same as the others, *tweezers*," Miss Pinkham explained.

"I know, Miss Pinkham. Would you please use it in a sentence?"

Herbie knew Annabelle was stalling. She wasn't sure.

"Of course. He used the tweezers to get the splinter out."

Annabelle softly cleared her throat. Then she resnapped one of her rainbow barrettes. "Tweezers . . ." She said it over and over in her mind. Did it end with an *-er* or *-or?* She wasn't sure. She couldn't remember seeing the word anywhere. She thought it started with two *e*'s, but did it end with one? It was a 50-50 chance. "t-w-e-e-z . . ." and then she paused.

The class watched and waited. They were staring at Annabelle's lips.

". . . o-r-s." Annabelle finished spelling the word.

"Incorrect."

The boys jumped out of their seats and cheered.

Miss Pinkham clapped her hands three times. "JUST A MINUTE!"

Everyone sat quietly back down in their chairs.

"Herbie Jones MUST spell the word correctly for the boys to win."

Annabelle broke out in a smile. How could Herbie spell *tweezers* if she couldn't?

Miss Pinkham asked Herbie to step forward. "Spell *tweezers*," she said.

Herbie couldn't wait. "T-w-e-e-z-e-r-s."

Miss Pinkham double-checked her list. "Correct!" she called out.

"YAHOO!" shouted the boys, and they lunged at Herbie.

Annabelle walked slowly back to her seat.

When Herbie got to his, she leaned over and said coldly, "You MUST have cheated, Herbie Jones. You knew that word was going to be given. Tweezers was NEVER on any of our spelling lists, and not once was it in any of our stories. How could you have known?"

Herbie pulled out his Trusty Tweezers. "I got lucky. Remember these? The word *tweezers* is

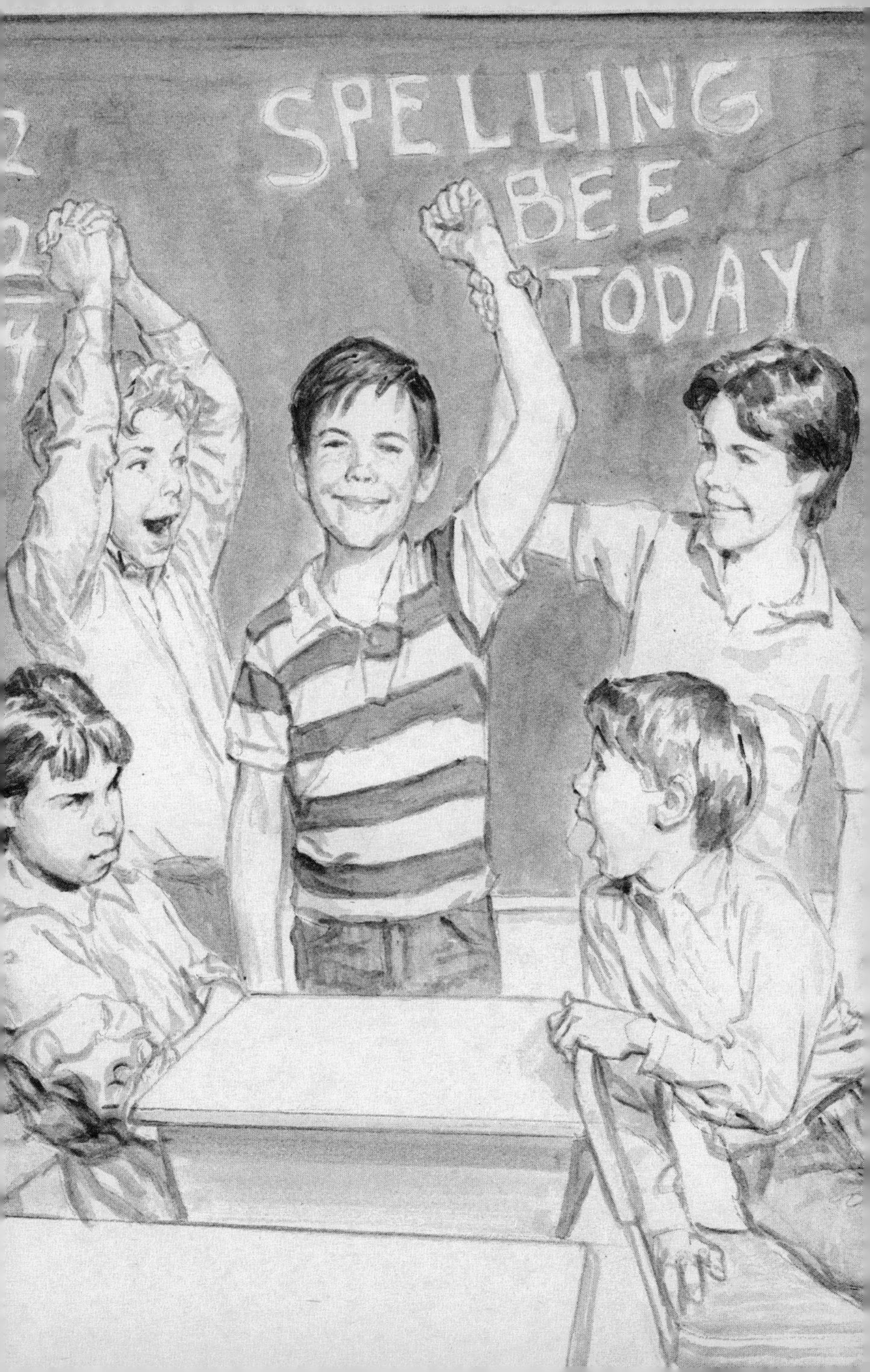
SPELLING
BEE
TODAY

printed right on the side, here. I've been looking at that word for two years."

The picture of the fish with a hair in it came to Annabelle's mind. EEYEW! she thought.

"Herbie Jones, I'll never ever be your girlfriend again as long as I live!" Annabelle took out her ALH memo cube and penciled in H-e-r-b-i-e with a check mark after it.

Herbie leaned on his elbows. "That's the nicest thing you've ever said to me."

"It is, huh?" Annabelle flared her nostrils. She made another check. This time it was in red crayon. "What do you think about that?" she asked.

Herbie didn't even hear her. He was thinking how great it was to be back in check city.